The Deep Black Pond at No. 12

Tammy and Jake find out about
Health and Sickness

Catherine Mackenzie

© Copyright Catherine Mackenzie 2004
ISBN 1-85792-7338

Published in 2004 by
Christian Focus Publications
Geanies House, Fearn, Ross-shire,
IV20 1TW, Scotland, UK.
www.christianfocus.com
email: info@christianfocus.com

Cover illustration by
Dave Thompson
Bee Hive Illustration
All other illustrations by
Chris Rothero
Bee Hive Illustration.
Printed and bound in Great Britian by
Cox and Wyman, Reading, Berkshire.

For Lydia, Esther, Philip, Lois and Jack

We love you!

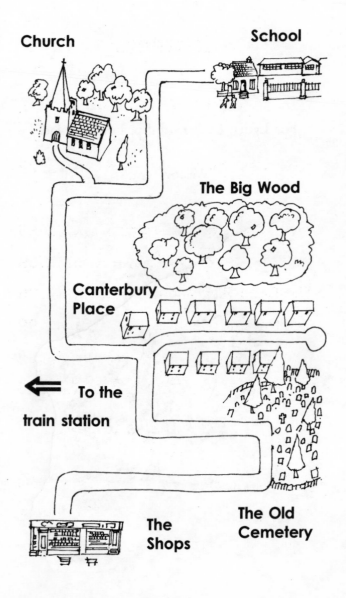

Church

School

The Big Wood

Canterbury
Place

← To the

train station

The
Shops

The Old
Cemetery

Contents

The Untidy Garden

Jake's boots squelched noisily as he pulled them out of the pile of mud at the back of Joyce's garden. Dogger sniffed excitedly. It was fun being in another garden, even if he wasn't allowed to do any of the digging.

"Yeuch," Tammy looked at her brother's feet and grimaced. "Your boots are covered in gunge."

Jake sighed. He took one look at his little, blonde-haired sister and smirked. She was dressed in a pair of pink Wellington boots that looked as if they had just walked out of a shoe shop. "Well that's one thing that's going to change," Jake said to himself.

"Come on Tammy – get to work. I know it's the first day of the Easter holidays but we said we'd help clean this pond. Joyce is Daniel's aunt and our kids' club teacher. She needs our help here."

Tammy smiled. "I'm really glad Joyce has moved to Canterbury place. She's fun to have around."

Jake nodded. "She'll also be a big help for Daniel and his mum. Daniel's mum still isn't feeling very well."*

Tammy then got down on her hands and knees and started to tug at some of the weeds.

Jake wiped the sweat from his forehead. He knew that he shouldn't complain but he couldn't help thinking about what he could be doing instead of gardening. "I could be playing football with Dave and Timothy!"

Timothy was one of Jake's best friends – but a few months ago his dad had been offered a new job in a town

*You can read more about this story in The Big Green Tree at No. 11

further north. But now and again Timothy was allowed to come to stay with his aunt who had a house not that far from Canterbury Place.

"Where is Daniel?" Jake asked.

Tammy wiped a smudge of dirt on her chin. "Didn't you hear? Joyce is taking Daniel's mum to the hospital today. The new medicine isn't working. It makes her feel sicker instead of better. Daniel might be a little late."

Jake looked concerned. He knew that Daniel had lots of good reasons for staying at home these days. "It must be tough for him. He spends a lot of time looking after his mum and Joyce is always taking her to the doctor or to the hospital. That's why she doesn't have time to work on this garden."

Tammy nodded as she struggled with a stubborn little weed. "And that's why we're doing it instead. It's one way to help Daniel and his mum and Joyce." Tammy gave a little cheer when the weed finally shot out of the soil. Then she remembered something. "Mum's going to bring over some snacks later."

Jake smiled. "She probably wants to make sure we're pulling out weeds and not flowers."

Tammy shrugged her shoulders. "That's not really a problem is it? I just can't see any flowers anywhere?"

From behind them Tammy and Jake heard a gentle chuckle. "I know the garden's in bad shape but it's not as bad as all that!" It was Mrs MacDonald, Tammy and Jake's mum. She was standing in the pathway holding a couple of cans of cola, two packets of crisps and a packet of sweets. "These are treats for later on. Don't eat them just yet. And Tammy I can see plenty of flowers on the hedge at the back - there just aren't any growing in the flower beds yet. We have to be patient. A lot of work is needed on this garden! Now, I have to call in at the office for an hour or so. I'll take Dogger back first though - he'll only start getting in your way." And with that Mrs MacDonald got hold of dogger's collar and headed for the gate. She called on her way out the gate, "Remember if you need anything ask Dad. He's working on the car at the moment but if he has time later on he might be able to come over and help you."

Jake nodded.

Some things never changed. Dad spent half his holidays working on their little green Morris Minor car. More things seemed to go wrong with that car than went right - a bit like this garden, Jake sighed as he heaved a large clod of mud into the wheelbarrow.

Just as Jake was putting the spade in for another shovel of dirt, Daniel nipped round the corner of the house and reached over to take hold of Jake's spade. "Sorry I'm late. Here, let me take a turn. You could do with a break."

Jake smiled, and went to help Tammy with the weeds.

"This gardening is harder work than I thought it would be. At home it's just a bit of weeding now and then."

Daniel was taller than Jake, though they were both in the same year at school. His dark hair and blue eyes were striking, but what made Daniel special was how he had changed from being someone Jake was scared of to someone who was a very good friend. Jake knew that it was God who had changed Daniel. It was amazing that next Sunday both Jake and Daniel were going to be doing a special story-time at the family service.

Daniel then rolled up his sleeves and threw a shovel of dirt into the barrow. He chatted as he worked. "This garden is untidy. Auntie Joyce almost decided to wait for another house – but then this one is so near us. If the people who lived here before had taken better care of the garden it wouldn't be so bad today. Look at it – I don't think I've ever seen so many weeds."

"Or thorns," said Jake

"Or mud," said Tammy.

The three youngsters sighed together before getting stuck into more of the weeds and thorns and mud.

Daniel Makes A Plan

An hour or so later, when the sun was higher in the sky, and Canterbury Place was busier and noisier, Tammy, Jake and Daniel put the shovels to one side and went to sit in the shade of the purple flowering hedge. They took the crisps and juice with them – Daniel had some fruit and a chocolate bar – so when they had shared it all out, they had quite a feast to look forward to.

Jake stopped to listen to the grumbling of the car from the garage across the road. Tammy sighed, "I don't think Dad's going to join us this morning." Jake scraped some of the dirt off his boots before taking another slug of cola. Daniel wiped his mouth with the end of his sleeve and burped. Jake sniggered and Tammy shot an angry look at both of the boys. "Manners!" she exclaimed, slightly shocked.

"Oh, Tammy!" Jake sniggered again. "We're not at the kitchen table now.

Manners don't count when you're outside."

"That's rubbish and you know it." Daniel and Jake tried not to smile but they couldn't help themselves and burst out laughing as Tammy stomped off to get rid of the remains of their picnic. As she disappeared round the front, Daniel stretched out his legs and took a long look at the garden in front of him.

"What do you think, Jake? Does the garden look any different?"

Jake shrugged his shoulders. He had to admit it. For all the work they had been doing on the pile of mud and weeds, this garden didn't look that different from when they first started. It was still muddy, full of weeds and thorns and just as untidy.

"I suppose it is going to take us quite a while," Jake suggested.

"You're right – but I think what we need is a plan."

"Of course. Why didn't I see it. We've been doing bits and pieces and not really completing anything. Tammy has a project to work on over the holidays, so why don't we pack away the shovels and head over to my house. We can work on a plan while we have some lunch. My dad might give us some advice too."

So Daniel and Jake moved the gardening equipment into the shed and headed off across the road. An enthusiastic bark was heard over the fence of Tammy and Jake's house. Dogger was eager to welcome the boys back to No.11. "Doesn't your dog jump fences? He's really keen to see us, isn't he?"

Jake ruffled the family dog behind the ears and then tickled him on the tummy as Dogger slowly rolled over on to his back. "Dogger used to be able to

jump fences no problem. But he's not as fit as he used to be. We took him to the vet last month. His heart gets tired and he wheezes a bit. The poor old dog is getting stiff and sore. You're bones aren't as good as they used to be, are they, Dogger?"

But at the mention of bones Dogger completely misunderstood what Jake was talking about and jumped up – fairly quickly for an old dog – and toddled off to wait by the garage door. "That dog's too smart. He knows that Mum keeps the bones in the old fridge by the freezer. All I have to do is say the word and he heads off to the garage."

"Clever dog," Daniel smiled. "Is he allowed one?"

"Yes. Bones are good for a dog's teeth. It's like when we brush our teeth. If a dog chews a bone it keeps them clean and healthy."

The two boys opened the fridge and pulled out a nice chunky bone.

Dogger grabbed it between his jaws and made off for the back of the garden.

Jake and Daniel headed for the kitchen. Mum had left sandwiches and some salad for lunch. An instruction was stuck on the fridge door. "No more crisps – you've had plenty. If you're still hungry after lunch have an apple. There are plenty of them."

Jake raised his eyes to the ceiling but didn't make much fuss about it.

"Mum's on one of her healthy eating campaigns."

"But these sandwiches look good!" Daniel exclaimed, pulling out the plate and moving towards the table.

Jake hollered towards the garage

where his dad was still working on the car. "Dad! Lunch is ready. Are you?"

"Ready in a tick, Jake. My stomach is making such loud noises. I'm so hungry."

Jake laughed. "I thought that noise was the car engine." Mr MacDonald chuckled as he put away his dirty overalls and took a seat at the kitchen table.

Tammy put out some cutlery and then Mr MacDonald asked Daniel to give thanks for the food.

Daniel beamed. "Sure, Mr MacDonald." He paused, closed his eyes, then began.

"Dear God, thank you for this food. Help us to please you. Thank you for friends and family and for your love. Amen."

Jake, Tammy and their dad all joined in with a loud Amen as well. Tammy passed round the sandwiches and salad and Jake smiled at his dad who smiled back at him. Yes, it certainly was amazing, how God had changed Daniel. Jake leaned back in his chair and looked at his friend who was chatting away and smiling. Tammy was laughing at his jokes. Jake's dad was enjoying a sandwich while looking at Daniel's notebook with his plans for the garden.

Jake was just about to peer over Daniel's shoulder to look at the notes when a question suddenly popped into his mind. It was a tricky one. Not one that he could answer very easily. "How come Daniel is so happy these days? I know that God's changed him and that he's a Christian now – but Daniel's mum is so ill. She doesn't seem to be getting any better. What is it that is making Daniel so happy? Why is it that God still hasn't healed his mum? I'm sure Daniel is praying for her to be made better – I know I am – so why hasn't anything changed?"

And as Jake looked at Daniel's plans and schedule for the garden he wondered if, perhaps, he could learn something from Daniel. "If I keep an eye on Daniel I might find out his secret."

What next for the Garden?

Jake and Daniel were up early and in the garden by eight o'clock. Daniel had a notebook in one hand, a pencil tucked behind his ear and some coloured felts and crayons sticking out of his pocket. His note book was full of plans and diagrams. It looked quite colourful. 'Perhaps the garden will be colourful one day,' Jake hoped. He had to admit that Daniel's plan made a lot of sense. They would get the weeds out first – pulling them out of the borders and from in between the paving slabs. There actually were some plants and even a cluster of crocuses and snowdrops poking through the earth. "If we clear the dead branches the sun will get through to the plants and help them grow," Daniel decided.

"But what about the pond?" Jake asked doubtfully. "That looks really horrible. We dug so much of that mud away yesterday – but it still looks bad."

"I think we should do the weeds first – as that's the easier job. Tammy can help too, then when it's time to do the pond we can let her do her project. She's really too young to be digging ponds like this. It's too hard for her."

"It is not!" Tammy had arrived. "I am not too young and it is not too hard. I can do any job that you boys can do."

Jake nodded and Daniel apologised. To prove her point Tammy marched over to the garden shed to drag out one of the spades. She was only just taller than it. Jake knew she wouldn't be able to carry it far. "Tammy, wait," he called out.

"We'll do the pond later. There's no digging today. Come and look at Daniel's plans for the garden and then you can help with the dead branches."

Tammy was relieved. The spade really had been too heavy. But she wasn't going to tell the boys that! But shifting the dead branches was hard work too and everyone felt hot and tired by lunchtime. When they wandered back across to No. 11 Mum was there to meet them.

"Leave your boots at the door and come and sit down," she ordered.

Jake sniffed as he sat down at the table. Pizza was a favourite. The grace was said and they all tucked in.

"You boys were out early," Mr MacDonald smiled as Jake and Daniel finished their pizza and eagerly accepted seconds. "I was so impressed that I think I'll give you a hand tomorrow."

Tammy then asked a question.

"Are we going to have Bible time now or later?"

Mum sipped her cup of tea.

"Well during the holidays things don't happen at the same time as usual, but I think we should still pray together in the morning and at night. Perhaps today, though, we could have Bible time after lunch instead. Would that be all right? Daniel can stay and join us if he likes."

Daniel swallowed the last mouthful of his pizza. "That would be cool Mrs MacDonald. We don't do that at home. I think my mum prays but I don't think Dad has ever gone to church."

Mrs MacDonald reached over and

squeezed Daniel on the shoulder. "Well, you're welcome to come to our house for prayer anytime. In fact," Mrs MacDonald's face lit up in a big smile, "I've had an idea!"

Mr MacDonald grinned. "Watch out! Mum's had an idea!"

"I mean it, Daniel should join in our family Bible times over Easter. You're here most of the time anyway. We'll have one at breakfast and then one at teatime before you go home. Tammy, go and get the Bible please. I think we're starting a new story today."

Tammy took the Bible off the shelf

 where it had been placed the night before. "What are we reading today, Dad?" she asked

"Well, let's see." Mr MacDonald, put on his spectacles and began to turn the pages. "Let's read about Jesus healing people."

"That sounds cool," Tammy smiled.

"Yes, Tammy. You see Jesus wants us to know how powerful he is. Jake, when Jesus calmed the storm, what was he more powerful than?"

"Water?" Jake replied.

"Yes. He calmed the waves and wind.

He even made fish swim into fishing nets. All these things belong to ..."

"Nature. Jesus had power over nature," Daniel exclaimed.

"Exactly. When he cured lepers what was he showing his power over?"

"Disease!" exclaimed Tammy.

"And when he raised a girl back to life, what did he show he had power over then?"

"That would be death. Yes?"

"Absolutely right. But Jake, can you tell me what was the most powerful thing that Jesus did?"

Jake thought for a little before

answering. "It's when Jesus rose from the dead after the crucifixion."

"What else did he do there?"

"He defeated Satan and saved God's people from their sins. It's because he bled and died on the cross that we can go to heaven when we die."

"Excellent answer. So when we see Jesus doing these miracles in the Bible we see God's power at work. The story we'll read today is about the daughter of Jairus. We aren't told her name, but we do know the name of her father ... and he was one of the people that Jesus was trying to teach in this story."

"What was he trying to teach him, Dad?" Jake asked, curious.

"Well, the story is in Mark chapter 5. Jairus came to ask Jesus to heal his twelve-year-old daughter who was sick and about to die. Jesus agreed to go and they left immediately for Jairus' house. But on the way a large crowd slowed them down. In the crowd there was a woman who had been bleeding for twelve years. She had been sick for every single year that Jairus' daughter had been alive. She'd tried many doctors and had spent all her money. But instead of getting better she got worse. When

 she saw Jesus she thought, "If I could only touch his clothes I would be healed." Gently she reached out and touched the edge of his cloak. Jesus knew that someone had touched him. He felt power going out of him. The woman knew something too – as soon as she touched Jesus she was better. Jesus asked out loud, "Who touched me?" The woman told Jesus the truth. Jesus turned to her and said, "Your faith has healed you. Go in peace." But just then a man arrived from Jairus' house.

"The girl is dead. Don't trouble Jesus any more."

But Jesus told Jairus not to be afraid but to believe. He went to Jairus' house and took Jairus and his wife and three disciples into the girl's room. He told the girl to get up. Immediately the dead girl came back to life. Everyone was astonished. Jesus told her parents to get her something to eat."

"That's amazing!" Tammy exclaimed. "Jesus healed two people that day. But what did he teach Jairus?" she asked.

"Jesus wanted Jairus to believe and not to be afraid. Jesus had a better

plan. He was going to bring Jairus'
daughter back to life."

Jake sat back and thought. "Why
doesn't he have power over Daniel's
mum's illness?" And as Mr MacDonald
put the Bible away Jake prayed that
somehow God would sort out the mess
of questions that were inside his head.

Football and a Shock

After lunch and Bible time Daniel and Jake wondered about going back across the road to do some more of the gardening, but Mrs MacDonald didn't agree.

"I think it's great that you are so keen to help Joyce, but you've worked hard this morning. I think you boys should go and have some fun. Go and see if Timothy and Dave want a game of football or something. I'm going to help Tammy with her project this afternoon. We're going to go into town to pick up one or two things first. Your father is still working on that pathetic car! So you're both free agents if Daniel's dad is all right with that."

Jake was just about recovering from the fact that Mum had called the Morris Minor 'that pathetic car' when he realised that Daniel was now filling her in on what was happening with his mum.

"She's still in hospital. The doctors are testing her with a new medicine. Auntie Joyce is staying with her and then swapping with Dad on Friday. It's a shame, but Mum and Dad won't be able to come and hear me give my story at the family service. I was hoping that Dad might have made it. I'd love it if he came to church."

Mrs MacDonald nodded. "Well, that's something to pray about. I'd love it too if your parents came to church."

Daniel smiled and picked up his dirty boots. "I'll take these home and then we can go and find Dave and Timothy."

Jake nodded his head as Daniel ran down the road towards No. 17. Jake turned to his mum who was looking anxiously at Daniel as he ran on. "I hope everything turns out all right."

"Do you mean about Daniel's mum?"

Jake's mum looked at him. "Well, yes, I really hope she gets better. But I was really thinking of something else."

Jake looked at his mum astonished. "What do you mean? Surely the most important thing is that Daniel's mum gets better."

"Don't get me wrong, Jake," Mrs MacDonald said urgently. "I pray every night that Daniel's mum recovers, but the important thing is to pray that Daniel's parents would come to love and trust Jesus."

Mr MacDonald came to the door and reached over to ruffle Jake's hair. Mrs MacDonald sighed. "Well, at least his hair was untidy. Every time you do that it seems that I've just combed it."

They all laughed, and as soon as Jake heard the door of No. 17 slam he ran off to join Daniel.

"Timothy said he'd be at Dave's when I phoned him the other night. So we'll head over there and see if we can get a couple of games in before the afternoon's over."

Tammy waved at them as they disappeared round the corner. Jake noticed that Dogger sat peering through the slats of the gate, his tongue panting, looking just a little sorry for himself.

"I think he wishes that he could come with us. Poor old dog."

That afternoon was spent kicking the ball around. Two of Dave's friends joined in the game and soon another four boys joined in. It was a good game and everyone played really well. At the end of the game Dave introduced the other boys. One took out a packet of cigarettes and offered them round. Jake noticed that they didn't offer them to Dave. Perhaps they knew that he didn't smoke. Timothy took one. Daniel didn't, and then they offered one to Jake. "No. I don't smoke," Jake muttered, glaring at Timothy. "What an idiot," Jake thought. "If he doesn't know how bad smoking is for you all he needs to do is ask Daniel. Both his parents smoked. His mum is ill and his dad coughs all the time." When the other boys had left, Jake, Dave and Daniel all turned to Timothy. Dave had a hurt look on his face. Daniel was surprised. Jake was furious. "What are you doing, Timothy?" he yelled. "Smoking is really bad for you. You won't get into the Youth Football League with a smoker's cough."

"Well I don't have one. And none of the smokers I know have one either..."

"They don't have one yet," muttered Daniel, who turned away and headed off towards the park gates.

Dave looked at Timothy. "I'm not

going to lecture you. You know what that stuff does to your body. They don't put cancer warnings on the packets for fun. But I think it's time we went home. I'll see you tomorrow, Timothy."

Timothy just shrugged and breathed out another cloud of cigarette smoke. Jake stomped off home angrily.

"I can't believe Timothy would do something so stupid! What an idiot! Some best friend. He's changed since he left here."

Just as Jake turned to go round on to Canterbury Place he noticed Daniel sitting on the wall outside his home.

Jake jogged up to meet him. "Are you coming to our house for tea?" Daniel looked up. "Yes. Your mum asked me. Dad says it's OK. We were only having chips tonight."

Jake felt a little jealous. "I wish we were having chips. Mum says they're full of fat and salt and things."

"She's right. Chips clog up your heart. The Americans call them fries. My dad serves chips with everything but it gets a bit boring after a while."

"Well, my mum's really into healthy eating so it will be baked potatoes, salad and chicken. I saw the ingredients in the fridge. At least I got pizza at lunchtime. Mum says that pizza is not too bad for you as long as there's loads of vegetables with it. And Mum isn't cooking green beans tonight so I should be thankful for that."

Daniel laughed. Everyone knew how much Jake hated green beans. "You and your green beans. You should try them some day. They're not that bad But that friend of yours, I didn't think he'd be a smoker."

Jake grimaced. "I didn't either.

Timothy's changed since I last saw him. I don't know what's happened."

Daniel nodded. "He probably got in with the wrong crowd. I did once, before I met you and Dave. Sometimes you'll do anything to fit in with people. I did lots of things, like bullying and stealing even, but I never smoked. I knew what it really did to people."

Jake sighed. If Daniel knew this then why didn't Timothy?

Questions and Questions

Jake had been right about the baked potato, salad and chicken. But mum also had a pudding for dessert. Mum announced that, "Going on a diet doesn't mean you cut out all tasty food. This is actually low in fat!" Jake smiled at this. Perhaps healthy eating wasn't going to be so bad.

After the dishes were put away Mum and Dad agreed that the family could watch some television for a while. "If there's nothing interesting on we'll switch it off. Are we agreed?"

Tammy and Jake nodded and Dad agreed. "We've got to be careful about what we eat and what we watch."

An advert came on where a young woman was smoking a cigarette. Others told the girl how smoking had made them ill, and put them in hospital. Another advert showed a very skinny young girl dancing around wearing some make-up.

Another advert urged them to buy a big burger and chips, and then they'd get another one free. When the final advert told them about a brand new way to lose weight – Mum just laughed out loud and Dad turned the TV off.

"TV programmes can be rubbish but the adverts can be just as bad. One advert tells you to eat a huge burger full of fat and then the next advert is telling you how to lose weight."

Mrs MacDonald laughed, "And did you see that skinny girl dancing around. That advert was trying to make us think that if we buy that make-up we'll look as beautiful as her. But a lot of the time they use computers to make someone look beautiful on T.V. Adverts can be very dishonest. You've got to be careful about what you watch. TV can be just as bad an influence as bad friends. In fact, the only advert that was any use was the first one warning about smoking."

Jake's mum looked across at him and Daniel. "You'll be getting pressure from other kids soon enough to do things like smoke cigarettes. I hope you never start something like that."

At this Jake and Daniel looked up. But Mrs MacDonald went on. "Our bodies are gifts from God. We should look after them."

Jake shifted uncomfortably on his seat. His dad looked at him. "What's up, Jake? You haven't smoked have you?"

"No way! I've never smoked and I won't either." Jake then told his parents about what had happened that afternoon.

Jake's Mum sighed. "I spoke to Timothy's mum on the phone a few weeks ago. She mentioned that he'd made some friends. It looks as if these friends aren't good friends after all."

Jake's dad reached over for the Bible. "Come on guys – let's read God's word and pray about this."

Tammy spoke up then, "Are we going to read about another miracle, Dad?"

"No, Tammy," Mr MacDonald said. "I think we'll leave that until tomorrow. There are a few verses of Psalms and Proverbs that I want to read to you. The book of Psalms is a Book of poetry

 mostly written by King David."

"He was the one who killed the Philistine giant Goliath when he was just a young boy," Tammy explained.

"Yes, and this is what God told him to say about wicked people and good people. 'Blessed is the man who does not walk with the wicked or stand beside sinners or sit beside people who mock the Lord. The man who delights in God's law and thinks about it day and night is like a tree planted by streams of water. It grows fruit in the right season and its

leaf does not wither. Whatever this man does is a success. But the wicked are like the dust that the wind blows away. That is why they will not be able to stand when it comes to the judgment day. They will not be able to stand with the righteous people. For the Lord looks after the righteous and knows where they are but the wicked will perish."

"Mr MacDonald," Daniel asked, puzzled. "What does that mean?"

"Well, there's a lot to learn here,

Daniel. Look at the first verse and pick out the first action word."

"Yes, that's easy. It's 'walk'."

"Jake what about the second one?"

"That would be 'stand'."

"And Tammy – what about the third?"

"That's 'sit'," Tammy exclaimed.

"This verse is telling us that someone who obeys God is going to be blessed, or happy. He is going to be like a strong, healthy tree growing beside clean, fresh water. Look at the tree in the garden. It's healthy and strong and useful. If you obey God you will be useful to him and live a life that is strong and good.

To be like this you shouldn't let wicked people make decisions for you. You should not become like them. Look at the action words again – 'Walk, Stand, Sit'. If two people walk together they might know each other – but if you see someone standing beside, or even sitting beside, someone then you know that they like spending time together. God is telling us to make sure we don't spend too much time with people who are sinning. If people sin we should tell them about Jesus. If we ignore their sin, sooner or later we might think that the sin isn't too bad after all. Then we might think that there is no harm in trying it for ourselves, and before you know it you are trapped by that sin and have been sucked into a life of disobeying God."

Jake nodded his head. Daniel looked worried, "But what if you are living with someone who doesn't love God?"

Jake's mum leaned over to speak to Daniel. "That is when people need to pray for you. Your parents don't love God yet, but what you have to do is show them how lovely God is. Obey God and pray that he will show you the right things to do."

Mr MacDonald then went on to read some more verses. "Before Daniel heads home I want us to look at Proverbs chapter 3 where it says, 'Do not be wise in your own eyes; worship God and turn away from evil. This will bring health to your body and nourishment to your bones.' It's important that you learn to turn away from evil. You did that today. That was good. But remember there will always be things to tempt you. As you grow up the devil will try and tempt you with other sins. Some of these sins may even kill you if you don't turn away from them. You must trust in God with all your heart and obey him. He knows what you should do."

Mr MacDonald put the Bible on the shelf and turned to Jake. "It's Jake's turn to pray tonight, I think. Let's all bow our heads."

Jake took a deep breath and began, "Dear God, thank you for the Bible. Help us to obey you. Help us to be good examples. Teach Timothy how to make the right choices. Please make Daniel's mum better." Jake took another deep breath and continued. "Thank you, God, for Mum and Dad and that they show us how to love you. Help us to be good Christians. Help us to please you. Amen."

As Jake snuggled under his bedclothes that night he listened to the wind in the branches of the big green tree. Even though he had so many questions he knew that he could trust God to have the answers. He was so glad that he was learning more and more about God every day.

Amazing things

The following morning Jake pulled on his jeans when he heard a well-known whistle outside the window. Peeking through his curtains he saw Daniel outside waving. Jake waved back and then looked at the clock. "Daniel's early," he gasped, "It's half past seven! We haven't even had breakfast yet."

Jake rushed down the stairs and caught the smell of bacon from the kitchen. "Mum likes to make a special effort when visitors are here."

The calendar on the wall said it was Wednesday. There were only five more days before school went back and Dad would return to work. It had been nice having him around. Jake was really pleased that his dad would help them in the garden.

Daniel started to chat almost as soon as he got in the door, and he was soon telling Jake's mum about how Joyce had phoned his dad the other night and how he was practicing for the family service next week. Jake was impressed with how Daniel wasn't letting his disappointment get him down. "I'd be really upset if my parents couldn't make it to the service. But at least Joyce will be there," Jake thought to himself.

Jake's dad gulped down his first cup of coffee before tucking into his bacon, egg and tomato.

Mum quietly pointed out that the egg was poached and the bacon and tomato were grilled. Jake smiled. It didn't matter. Breakfasts like this always tasted good if Mum cooked them.

Tammy was the last to join them. Her hair was unbrushed and her eyes looked tired. Mum sighed and quickly took out a brush from the kitchen drawer and tidied Tammy's golden curls. "Breakfast is going to be at half eight tomorrow and Friday. I don't want to be sending you back to school for a rest. Holidays are supposed  to be fun – not exhausting!"

Once everyone had eaten, Mrs MacDonald handed out some oranges.

"You're supposed to eat five portions of fruit and veg every day," she announced. Jake didn't mind the orange, he quite liked them. But he did wonder if this new fruit and veg rule might just be an excuse for green beans at dinner time!

Once the fruit was eaten and the dishes cleared away Jake's mum sat down with the Bible on her lap.

"Today's story is about a blind man who was given back his sight by Jesus. Tammy, can you find John chapter 9?"

Tammy squished up beside her mum and turned some pages. The Book of John was in the New Testament towards the end of the Bible. In her mind she

went through the first few Books –
Matthew, Mark, Luke then John. She
soon found it and turned the pages until
she arrived at a big number 9. "Got it!"
she announced, very pleased.

"Well done! Now listen to the story.
Jesus is walking along the road with
his disciples when they see a man
who had been blind from the very day
he was born. When the disciples saw
the man they thought that he must
have done something very bad for
God to make him blind. "Perhaps his
parents sinned? What do you think,
Jesus?" They asked. Jesus turned to

them and said,

"This man isn't blind because he sinned or his parents sinned. He is blind so that the work of God can be shown in his life."

Jesus then bent down and spat on the ground. He mixed some mud with his saliva and put this on the man's eyes. "Go and wash in the pool of Siloam." The man obeyed, and when he came back he could see!

When the Pharisees heard about this

they began to ask the man who had been blind all sorts of questions. But he said. "Why do you want to hear it again? Do you also want to become Jesus' disciples."

The Pharisees got very angry. They hated Jesus and wanted others to hate him too. But the man turned to them and said, "Jesus opened my eyes. We know that God listens to those who obey him. I was born blind and Jesus gave me back my sight. Nobody has heard of that before. If Jesus did not come from God he would not be able to do these wonderful things."

The Pharisees replied, "You sinful man! Don't tell us what to do! Get out of here!"

Tammy folded her arms and exclaimed, "Those rotten old Pharisees! They never listened."

"You're right, Tammy. But the man who was born blind knew the truth. He knew that Jesus was from God because of the wonderful things he did. That was one of the reasons there were so many miracles done in the Bible times. Jesus wanted to show the people how powerful God was and that he was God's son."

Jake scratched his head and then

asked his mum one of the questions that had been bothering him.

"Why doesn't God do miracles today?"

Jake's mum looked across at her husband. "I think he does do miracles Jake. What's the most amazing thing that God has done for you?"

Jake thought, and then he realised what his dad was getting at. "He saved me from my sin. He made me into someone who loves God."

"That's right. And God still heals people. He gives people skills to use which help people get better. There is always a reason for the things that God does. Daniel read verse four. Why was it that the man had been born blind in the first place?"

Daniel looked at the verse. "The man was born blind so that God could show how powerful he was. Does that mean that my mum is sick so that God can show us his power when he heals her?"

Jake's dad rubbed his chin thoughtfully. "You might be right. If your mum gets better we must thank God for that. The Bible tells us that he is the God who heals. But I know a story about a girl who was in an accident. She was told that she would never walk again or use her hands. This girl was angry at God. She asked him to make her better, but he didn't. However, as she prayed to God and listened to what he had to say in the Bible, she began to realise that God's plans are not like our plans."

Tammy looked confused. "What do you mean, Dad? Did God not want to make this girl better?"

"Yes he did. But what he wanted most of all was to make this girl love him with all her heart. And he wanted to use her in his special work."

"What was this girl's name?" Daniel asked.

"Her name was Joni,"* Mr MacDonald replied. "She couldn't walk or use her hands, but in the end she knew that God's plan was the best plan. Joni helped other people who had been in accidents and couldn't walk. She told them about Jesus and how he loved them. God could have healed Joni. That would have been amazing. But instead he helped Joni to love him and he helped her to do a really important job for him. That was more amazing."

*You can read more abour Joni's story in 'Swimming against the Tide' and 'Ten Girls who changed the world'.

Jake wasn't so sure, "God could have healed her too. Why didn't he do that later on?"

"Remember, God's plans are not like our plans. We might think we know what is best, but often we are wrong."

Jake's mum then interrupted, "Do

you remember when we talked about Grandpa dying."*

Jake nodded, "That was before I was born. His body is buried in the cemetery along the road."

"That's right. Before Grandpa died I prayed for him to get better. But when he died I knew that he was better. When those who love Jesus go to be with him, all their pain goes away. And when it's the right time God will give his people new bodies that will last forever. Joni does amazing things for God. She speaks about Jesus to thousands of people. She raises money to buy wheelchairs for poor

*You can read more about this story in The Big Green Tree at No. 11

people. She paints beautiful pictures holding the brush in her mouth instead of her hands, and she writes books. She says that she is really looking forward to meeting Jesus. She is going to be able to run and walk and dance again, and she is going to be in heaven with Jesus whom she loves best."

Daniel nodded, but looked sad and lonely. Mrs MacDonald gave him a hug.

Daniel smiled, "I'm still praying that Mum gets better. But I'm also praying that Dad will love God too. Sometimes I think that my dad will never come to church. He laughed when he saw me reading my Bible the other night."

Jake's dad then prayed for his family and Daniel's parents too, and when everyone was getting their coats to go across to Joyce's garden Jake wondered which would be more amazing – Daniel's mum getting better or Daniel's dad going to church. "I suppose that both would be pretty cool," he said, as he gave Dogger a scratch behind the ears.

The Deep Black Pond

"Right then troops. Let's look at this plan of yours and get digging." Jake's dad was dressed in his dark green Wellington boots, some scruffy jeans and an old jacket and cap. Everyone else was wrapped up warm because of a slight chill in the air. Mr MacDonald soon started giving out instructions.

"I'm going to follow Daniel's plan here and give everybody different jobs to do. Tammy, you take this dustpan and brush and sweep the path at the top of the garden. I can see you've done a good job of that part of the garden already."

Jake and Daniel looked at where they had been working the other day. Mr MacDonald was right. That part was looking a lot better.

"Jake, you start work on the weeds. Daniel and I will start on the pond."

Everybody went off to do his or her own job. Tammy sang some songs while she was brushing up the dirt and the time went very quickly. Jake carefully took the rake and gently dragged it over the soil, loosening it up a little and getting rid of some stones before lifting up the weeds and putting them in the bin. Mr MacDonald came over to inspect Jake's work. "Well done, son! That's a good job. Come over and look at the pond."

Jake went over and was astonished at how much mud Daniel and his dad had shifted. It was definitely looking more like a pond now. Tammy ran over and jumped right in. But as there was no water she didn't get too messy!

"I hope we can have frogs and goldfish in this pond," she said excitedly.

"Suggest that to Joyce when she gets back on Friday. But I thought I saw a frog already this morning. Keep an eye out for it, Tammy. Now let's see what kind of food Mum has given us."

Jake sighed, "It's probably lettuce, carrots and water. She's still on that diet!"

But Jake was wrong. Mum had packed the rucksack with some bananas and apples, a large bottle of fruit juice and some tumblers as well as several large chunks of her home made fruit loaf.

"Fantastic!" Daniel exclaimed, tucking into a banana and pouring out some juice.

"Get stuck in everyone," Jake's dad called out. And everybody did.

As they were all munching away Mr MacDonald began to tell a story.

"When I was a youngster my parents went on holiday with my sister and me.

We stayed in an empty house that belonged to some friends of ours.

When we arrived there was a little box by the door with a treasure map and a long list of clues. Clue number one was, 'In the garden by the shed you'll find it in a little bed'. What do you think that meant?"

Tammy and Jake were puzzled, but Daniel knew the answer almost straight away. "Sometimes people call a piece of ground with some flowers in it a flower bed. So the next clue must have been in the flower bed by the shed. Am I right?"

"Exactly," Mr MacDonald smiled. "The next clue was, 'You would think this house was painted bright – but there isn't a single colour in sight.'"

"That's difficult," Daniel said.

But Tammy was looking over the fence at next-door's garden. "It's a greenhouse, Dad, isn't it?"

"Well done, Tammy! A greenhouse is a shelter for plants like tomatoes that need a bit more warmth. It's called a greenhouse because green things grow in it, not because it is painted green."

"Give us another clue, Dad?" Jake asked.

"All right then. Let's see if I can remember. 'There isn't a roof, but it is a home. There isn't a door but you could go in. It might be wet but it could get dry. Look at it. You'll see yourself'. Now tell me why?"

Jake looked very puzzled and so did the others. "It must be something in the garden, and something lives in it."

"You're getting warm, Jake," smiled his dad.

"If I looked at it I would see myself. I know. The pond!"

"Got it in one! Fish might live in it. You could go in it if you wanted to, like

Tammy did a moment ago. But if it was full of water and you looked in it you would see your reflection."

"That's really cool, Dad," Tammy laughed. "Did you find the treasure in the end?"

"Yes we did. It was a jam jar full of pennies and a couple of pound notes. We saved the money for buying sweets and souvenirs at the end of the holiday. But one thing I remember about that garden was that it was even untidier than this one.

My dad taught me a

little about weeding during that holiday, but I think it is a lesson that you've already learned."

"How's that?" Tammy asked.

"Well, you've taken the whole weed out – roots and all – and not just the stalk. Why is that so important?"

Tammy explained, "If you leave the roots in, the weed grows back. You must take the roots out to get rid of the whole weed."

"That's right. Weeds are just like sins. Weeds make a garden look untidy and they stop flowers growing. Sin makes your life a mess too. It can stop you learning about God and doing good things. If you want to make your garden healthy you have to get rid of weeds. If you want to make your life healthy you have to get rid of sin and you have to get rid of all sin. You might try and stop sinning on your own but that won't work. You have to ask Jesus to help you beat sin. That's the only way to get rid of it completely. When you trust in Jesus God agrees to throw away all your sin. When he looks at you all he sees is the perfect Lord Jesus who died for you and who rose again."

Tammy put her dustpan and brush

back in the shed and looked at all the dirt on her boots, "This garden wouldn't be so untidy if someone had looked after it."

"That's right, Tammy," her dad sighed. "If someone had done a little bit of work every day and kept on top of things then the garden would be much healthier. Remember when you're reading your Bible and praying to God you should do it every day. Learn about God bit by bit. That way you'll become a strong and healthy Christian. If you get lazy and don't work at your Christian life things will get difficult. If someone had kept working in this garden it wouldn't be such hard work now. If you keep working at learning about God you'll always be ready to do your best for God."

Jake's Dad packed the remains of the picnic back into the rucksack. He then looked at the pond and the rest of the garden. "Let's see if we can finish off the weeding before we head back over the road." So together Jake, Daniel, Tammy and Mr MacDonald started to pull out more weeds, roots and all.

Healthy and Happy

When the gardeners stopped before lunchtime they had gathered together a large pile of weeds. It didn't take them too long to get it all tidied away and then they went across to the MacDonald house for lunch.

When they opened the door Jake could smell spaghetti sauce. Mum called out from the kitchen, "Great! you're just in time. Come and tuck in. I've got to go out to work in half an hour. Tammy's friend, Nathalie, is here for lunch too. They're going to do their projects together. You boys could spend some time on your stories for the family service."

Jake and Daniel both thought this was a good idea, "We can go out on our bikes afterwards. What do you think?" Daniel asked.

"Excellent!" Jake exclaimed as he sat down at the table. "Did you get that new helmet from your dad?"

"Yes, I did. It's the same colour as

the bike – dark blue with silver and red stripes. Quite cool."

Jake smiled. He remembered how jealous he'd once been of Daniel's bike. And he still wanted a bike just like it – but he didn't mind seeing Daniel ride it anymore and sometimes Jake and Daniel swapped bikes for a bit.

Once lunch was over Jake and Daniel went up to Jake's bedroom to work on their stories.

"Joyce said that we have to talk about something that God has helped us with. What are you going to do, Daniel?"

Daniel chewed the end of his pencil. "I think I'm going to talk about how God is helping me with my mum. Your  parents talked about how God's plans are different from our ones. I'm still hoping that God will make mum better, but he has been helping me to feel happy even when mum is sick."

Jake realised that this was what he had been puzzled about. "How is it that God's making you happy then?" he asked.

Daniel sat back against the bed and reached over for Jake's Bible. "I've been reading things in the Bible that make me feel peaceful. When I read what God is saying I know that he loves me and that I don't have to be afraid. He's going to be with me whatever happens. I asked your mum the other day if she could tell me some Bible verses to read. Can you find the Book of Jeremiah?" Daniel asked Jake.

Jake took the Bible and flicked through some of the Old Testament. Jeremiah was a hard Book to find. "If we turn to the front of the Bible it will give us the page numbers to look up. Here we are. Jeremiah starts on page 637. What chapter do you want?"

"J e r e m i a h chapter 29 verse 11. I read it last night."

Jake looked up the chapter and verse and began to read it out loud, "For I know the plans I have for you," says the Lord, "plans to help you and not to harm you, plans to give you a hope and a future."

Daniel nodded. "This means that whatever happens, God's plans are the best plans – because he loves me." Daniel looked over at Jake, "What are you going to do your story on?" he asked.

"I've no idea. I've got lots of things to thank God for. But I'm not sure if I should be speaking at church when I've so many questions to ask."

Daniel shrugged his shoulders. "Everybody's got questions. Questions are nothing new. You're not the only person who has them. Even preachers have questions, I'm sure."

"Maybe," Jake agreed. "I just hope I get a good idea soon about what I should say."

"Well, let's work on mine and then we'll go off on the bikes. That might clear your head a bit and give you a brilliant idea."

Jake agreed with Daniel's plan, and they both sat down to work out some words for Daniel to say.

Later on the two boys sped off down the woodland track, swerving around tree trunks and jumping over roots and puddles. Sometimes mud splashed up their trouser legs – but that was all part of the fun. They saw Dave in the distance walking home. He didn't stop so the boys carried on to the end of the wood.

"I didn't see Timothy with Dave, did you?" Jake asked Daniel.

"No. There was no sign of him. Do you want to head over to his aunt's house to see him?"

Jake nodded, and both boys cycled off. Timothy's aunt lived in a bungalow with two bedrooms. The door was round the side of the house. Jake pressed the buzzer and waited.

Timothy's aunt opened the door and smiled. "Sorry boys, but Timothy's not allowed out today. He has been grounded until his mum comes down at the weekend. You might see him at church on Sunday though."

Jake nodded, and said goodbye. "What has Timothy done now?" he wondered.

It didn't take them long to find out. As they pushed their bikes back along the road, Daniel spotted Dave at the corner. They both ran to catch up with him and Dave soon filled them in on what had happened.

"I knew he'd be found out sooner or later," Dave sighed. "His aunt was suspicious. I'm sure she must have smelt the smoke. But anyway, she was just about to put Tim's jacket in the wash when she discovered his packet of cigarettes in a pocket. She's furious! And so she should be. Tim has been really stupid these days. You should hear the way he goes on. He says he's been skipping school and  that he's even stolen sweets from the corner shop near his home."

"What should we do, Dave?" Jake asked, alarmed.

"Tim knows he is doing wrong. If we see him doing it again we should tell him it's wrong and then leave him. He is our friend but we shouldn't be around with him when he's doing all this stuff."

"But we should pray for him," Daniel said.

When they got back to No. 9 supper was soon on the table and Tammy had lots of news about her project. "We're nearly halfway through already. We're both learning about healthy eating and exercise."

"That's cool," said Daniel. "Your mum can help you with the healthy eating bit. I love eating at your house."

"There are lots of things you have to do to keep healthy though. You have to brush your teeth, get plenty exercise, wash yourself, drink plenty water. Nathalie and I exercised this afternoon too. We danced, went for a walk and Nathalie let me borrow her roller blades." Tammy was really this project.

Mr MacDonald smiled as he sat down at the table. "A healthy body, food to eat, clean fresh water to drink. God gives us lots of good gifts."

Good things and bad things

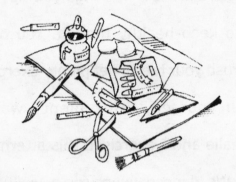

When the plates were all washed and stacked away, Tammy showed Jake and Daniel the project that she had been working on. Jake was impressed with all the pictures she had drawn. She had even made a list of all the food available in the kitchen cupboard. Tammy's list showed how many calories were in each kind of food, how much sugar, how much salt, and how many vitamins. Just as Tammy was showing the boys how much salt was in a packet of biscuits, Jake's dad got the Bible out once again. "Come on gang, it's Bible time. We are reading in Luke chapter 17. In this miracle one person does something that none of the others do. Try and work out what it is. It all happened when Jesus was on his way to Jerusalem. As he was going into a village ten men who suffered from the skin disease, leprosy, saw Jesus and called out to him. "Have pity on us!"

When Jesus saw them, he said, "Go and show yourselves to the priests." So the lepers headed off to find the priests. As they went they were all cleansed of their leprosy. One, when he saw that he was healed, came back praising God in a loud voice. He threw himself at Jesus' feet and thanked him.

Jesus asked the man, "Were not all ten of you cleansed? Where are the others? Get up, your faith has made you well."

"I know what the difference is!" exclaimed Tammy. "One man thanked Jesus and none of the others did."

"That's correct," said Mr MacDonald. "This teaches us to be thankful. We have already thanked God for our food tonight. But we have lots of things to thank God for, like our health, water to drink, and his word, the Bible."

Jake's mum noticed that he was a bit puzzled, "What are you thinking of, Jake?" she asked.

"Jesus said to the leper that it was his faith that had made him well. I thought it was Jesus that had done it?"

"Oh boy, that's a tricky question, Jake!" exclaimed his dad. "It was Jesus' power that healed the man. The man also believed in Jesus, but faith is a gift from God in the first place."

Jake was still full of questions though, "If the man hadn't had faith, would Jesus have healed him?"

"Another difficult question, son. But Jesus did heal people who didn't really believe in him. In John chapter 5 he heals a man who actually tries to get him into trouble by telling the Pharisees what Jesus had done."

"So why did Jesus heal that man?"

"Jesus was showing people what God is like. God is loving and he gives good things to people who love him and to people who don't. Jesus wanted to show this man how powerful God was. He wanted to tell him to stop sinning. But the man didn't listen."

"So if you love God and fall ill is it because you don't have a strong faith?"

"No. That's not true. God might want to show the world his power through your illness instead of through healing you. Do you remember the story of Joni?"

Jake remembered the story about the girl who hadn't been able to walk. "God helped her, but he didn't heal her."

"That's right. He helped her to love

him more. And even when she did, he still didn't heal her. That might have been because he could show other people how powerful he was by helping Joni cope with her problems instead of by taking them away. Sometimes bad things can actually turn out to be good things. Sometimes good things happen because bad things have happened first. Daniel, look at Galatians chapter 4 verse 13. What does Paul say there?"

"As you know it was because of an illness that I first preached about Jesus to you." Daniel read out and looked surprised. "That's a good thing that happened because a bad thing happened first."

"Exactly. Do you remember what happened in the story of Joseph?"

"He was sold as a slave by his brothers," Jake answered.

"But if he hadn't been sold as a slave he would not have been able to help all these people, and his family when the famine came. Joseph was eventually made the second most powerful leader in the whole land. Only Pharaoh was more powerful. That's how he managed to supply food to his family. During the famine he was in charge of Egyptian food distribution. But he wouldn't have been if he hadn't been sold as a slave first. So that's another example of God making a bad thing happen so that a good thing can happen later. Can you think of another one?"

Nobody answered. Then Mrs MacDonald spoke up. "I think I can. Jesus died on the cross so that we could be saved from our sins, and then he rose from the dead so that we can live in heaven with him forever. That's one very bad thing that happened so that two amazingly good things could happen afterwards."

Mr MacDonald nodded his head and explained, "Sometimes if we aren't healed from a disease, it is because God wants this bad thing to happen so that a good thing can happen later. Someone might see how you are patient even though you are ill. You could then tell them about how God helps you. Illness can sometimes make us stronger Christians. Sometimes God can make us thankful for a bad thing."

"That still doesn't make it nice," Tammy complained.

"You're right, Tammy. Illness and disease are awful things. And what we have to remember is that these bad things are here because of sin. Because all have sinned God has had to punish us. Part of that punishment is sadness and illness and getting tired and upset. We can ask God to help us and to heal us but we can't blame God for something that is our own fault, especially when God sent his son to earth to save us by dying on the cross. But that's enough for now guys. Daniel has to head home. Tammy, I think it's your turn to pray."

Tammy closed her eyes and bowed her head. "Dear God, thank you for food and water and healthy bodies and Jesus. Help us to love you and be your friends. We are sorry for our sins. Amen."

Later on, when Jake was brushing his teeth, he thought about all the questions he'd been asking.

"I suppose I'll always have questions," he muttered to himself. "Dad says that I might not get all the answers I want until I get to heaven."

Dad looked in on Jake before he went to sleep and ruffled his hair against the pillow. "You were full of questions tonight boy. I'm really pleased."

"Pleased?" Jake couldn't understand that. He thought that asking questions all the time meant that he was stupid.

"Of course I'm pleased!" Jake's dad exclaimed, "It's good to ask questions and to want to know more about God. And even though God doesn't give us the answers yet, he's glad that you're asking questions too. Keep reading the Bible, Jake, and God will teach you the right things to do. And keep praying for Daniel's mum. I know that God is going to do something good at the end of all this. We just don't know what he's going to do yet."

Jake nodded and closed his eyes, breathing a quiet prayer before he went to sleep.

"Please make Daniel's mum better. Please do something good for Daniel."

Good News and Bad News

Thursday came and went and then Friday. Daniel's Auntie Joyce was picked up from the train station. When she arrived at the house she was really pleased with all the hard work that they had done on the garden.

"It's wonderful!" she exclaimed. "I wouldn't recognise the place. And look at that pond! It's almost ready to put water in now. What do you think, Tammy? Should I put some fish in it?"

"Yes!" Tammy agreed. "I think you should ... and some frogs."

Joyce smiled, "A frog or two might be quite nice. What a good idea."

Daniel seemed happy too. His dad was going down to spend the weekend with Mrs Conner in the hospital and it looked as though she might be home next week. Joyce had agreed to drive Daniel to the hospital on Sunday after the family service. Daniel was looking forward to it.

"Does that mean that Daniel's mum is not going to be sick anymore?" Tammy asked.

"Not really," said Mum. "But the medicine is working, and she'll be able to come home. She really is feeling a lot better."

Joyce agreed with Jake's mum that Saturday as well as Sunday should be days of rest, and that they would all take some time off from the garden. Joyce even said they could take Friday off if they wanted, but Jake and Daniel decided to clear some more bushes and tidy up some flowerbeds.

Joyce smiled. "Well that shouldn't take you too long. How about you do that now and in an hour's time you can come with me to chose some plants at the garden centre?" Jake and Daniel thought this was a great idea. When they arrived there they were really impressed with all the plants and garden equipment.

"Wow!" Daniel gasped, when he saw a huge plant arrangement in the car park. "Wouldn't it be wonderful if our garden looked like that!"

Joyce looked at the colourful display and agreed. "I think these plants would look very good in the garden. But don't expect our garden to look like this next week. We'll have to be patient. Plants have to have time to grow."

Jake and Daniel shrugged their shoulders. Being patient was always difficult. But the two boys were soon enthusiastically helping Joyce to pick plants and shrubs. It was quite a difficult job. They had to use Daniel's garden plan to work out where the best place would be for some of the flowers. Some shrubs grew well in shady areas, some needed lots of sunshine. Eventually Joyce had a trolley full of plants and shrubs, and a good selection of seeds to plant.

"I'm looking forward to seeing this garden grow. I've had a good look at the soil and it's really healthy. I might even grow a few vegetables in that sunny patch by the window. I see they're selling lettuce seeds and radish seeds. I think I'll buy some."

When Joyce had made all her purchases, they headed back to the car to pack them away in the boot.

Back at Canterbury Place Daniel and Jake helped Joyce to move the plants to the shed. She gave them some water and took the seed packets inside to read up on what she was supposed to do. "Are you boys hungry?" she asked.

Jake smiled, "Mum says we're always hungry, but she told me to ask you and Daniel for lunch if you'd like."

"That's kind of her," smiled Joyce. "You go over then. Tell her I'll be along in a minute."

So Jake and Daniel headed across the road to see what Mrs. MacDonald was cooking for lunch. But as they came through the back door there was no sign of any cooking. In fact the house was really quiet. Then Jake heard Tammy crying in the sitting room.

Jake rushed through to the sitting room. Something really bad must have happened. "What is it, Mum? What's wrong?"

"Daniel, it's Dogger. Dad had to take him to the vet." Mum explained that when she and Tammy had come back from the shops, Dogger had been finding it hard to breathe. Then all of a sudden he collapsed on the floor.

Tammy burst into tears again. "I

want to pray for Dogger. Is it OK to pray for dogs?"

"Yes, I'm sure you can pray to God about anything that is bothering you." Mrs MacDonald then asked God to look after Dogger and to help Tammy and Jake not to feel too sad. An hour later Dad came back from the vet. "It's not good news. Dogger is really sick. The vet says that he will keep him overnight and give him some medicine, but he might not get better."

Jake felt a little tear trickle down his cheek. Tammy sniffed loudly. Just then the phone rang and Dad answered it.

 Jake could tell it was the vet on the other end. Dad was nodding and saying, "Yes, yes. I understand. Thank you for everything you did. I'll call round in a bit."

Jake didn't want to hear what Dad was going to say next.

"I'm afraid Dogger has died. The vet says that in the end his heart just gave up. The last time we took him to the vet he warned us that Dogger's heart was quite weak."

Tammy ran up to her room, sobbing.

Jake went out into the garden. He sat on the back step and looked at the big green tree in the corner with the old tyre swing. He wondered how many bones Dogger had buried in the garden over the years. Daniel came and sat beside him. Jake sighed. "I'm going to miss that old dog," he said.

Daniel nodded, "Me too. It's funny how he knew what the word 'bones' meant, isn't it?"

Jake laughed. Dogger had always been clever when

there was food around. They'd probably be discovering bones in this garden for years to come.

Just then the phone went again. Mum picked it up this time, and though she sounded a bit sad when she answered it, by the end of the conversation she was sounding really happy. "Oh that is good news, Mr Conner. I'm so pleased. Wait a minute and I'll put Daniel on the phone."

Daniel dashed into the kitchen and grabbed the phone from Jake's mum. She laughed and walked out to the garden to sit with Jake. "Well that's some good news after some bad," she said, giving Jake a hug at the same time. "Daniel's mum is getting home early. They're driving home tomorrow morning."

Jake looked up and smiled even though a tear was still in the corner of his eye. Tammy then joined them on the steps. Though she still looked upset she wasn't crying anymore.

Just then the MacDonalds heard a loud whoop of delight as Daniel came running out the door. "Dad is coming to church on Sunday, and Mum too. God has answered my prayers!"

That evening Dogger was buried in a corner of the garden right at the back of the big green tree. Tammy put a small stone on the top. Then they all went inside. Daniel had suggested that they might get another dog some day, but Jake didn't want to think about that. Dogger had been the best dog in the whole world. They would never get another dog as good as him.

Time for a break

Jake woke up on Saturday morning and could hardly believe that tomorrow was the day of the family service. He still hadn't made up his mind about what to say. But at least Saturday was a day off from gardening and so was Sunday. Both Tammy and Jake were pleased to have a day off, and Daniel was delighted that his mum would be coming home that morning. Daniel had spent the night at Joyce's and after breakfast he asked her if he could join Jake for the family Bible time at No.11. Joyce said that was a good idea and phoned over to check with Jake's mum if that would be alright.

"Of course. We'd love to have him. How about coming yourself, Joyce?"

Joyce agreed, and took a box of chocolate biscuits with her. "I can't remember when I last saw a chocolate biscuit," Jake muttered. Mum smiled, and handed him one from the box.

When it was time for the Bible reading Dad started by reminding them of the story of Joni once again.

"Remember how Joni had that accident that meant she couldn't walk. Someone who can't walk is paralysed. That was when I remembered that there is a story in the Bible about Jesus healing someone who was paralysed. It's in Luke chapter 5. One day when Jesus was in a house teaching the people, some men came along the road carrying a man on a mat, but because there was such a large crowd they couldn't get through the door to bring their friend to Jesus. But in Israel at that time most houses were made with flat roofs, and there was a flight of steps up the side of the house that led to the roof. The friends carried the paralysed man up the steps and laid him down on the roof. It was just above where Jesus was teaching. They began to scrape away at the roof and soon made a large hole. It was big enough to lower the man through, so that was what they did. Jesus turned to the man on the mat and said, "Friend, your sins are forgiven." But the Pharisees began to think bad thoughts about Jesus. "He's a sinful man to say that. Nobody can forgive sins but God." But Jesus turned to them and said, "Why are you thinking these things in your hearts? Which is easier – to say 'your sins are forgiven' or to say 'get up and walk'? But I am going to show you that I have the power to forgive sins..." and Jesus spoke to the paralysed man "Get up, take your mat and go home."

Immediately the man stood up, picked up his mat and went home, shouting and singing about how wonderful God was."

Jake wasn't sure what was more

difficult. To forgive someone's sin or to heal them. But then he realised something. When Jesus had forgiven sin he was actually doing something very wonderful. "God can change someone's body and make it better. But he can also change your soul and make you want to please him. That is amazing! And I've just had a great idea for the family service!"

The Family Service

Sunday morning was beautiful, but Jake still felt nervous when he went down for breakfast. It was strange not to see Dogger there, but Jake tried not to think about it just in case it made him cry again. After breakfast was over the MacDonalds piled into Dad's car and set off for church.

Jake smiled and waved at Daniel who was sitting beside his mum and dad. Both his parents were chatting to someone who was sitting beside them. It was Joyce. She called over to him, "Hi Jake. Good to see you. After the minister prays you're going to be the first to speak and then Daniel. Alright?"

Jake tried to swallow his nerves then remembered how Nehemiah had prayed a quick prayer to God when he was in trouble. "Please God, help," Jake whispered, and then he sat down. The minister was now at the front and the musicians had started to play. Soon it was time for Jake and Daniel to tell their stories.

The minister introduced them to the congregation and then Jake began. "I've got lots of things to thank God for. It's hard to know what to say. But I decided to do something different and it's all about the word 'Thanks'.

T stands for Truth. I thank God for the truth he has given us in his word.

H stands for Health. God gave me a body to look after as well as I can. I thank him for that. It means I can play football - which is great!

A stands for Ask. I can ask God for

what I need. When he gives me these things I must thank him for them.

N stands for Now. I must thank God now and always. Even when my dog has just died. I should still be thankful to God because he is good.

K stands for Kindness. God is full of kindness. He loves me.

S stands for Salvation. This is God's best gift. God has saved me from my sin. Jesus has done so much for us all. We should all give thanks."

As Jake sat down again he noticed that Daniel was now up the front.

"I want to thank God for something

that happened eight months ago, for something that happened this week, and for something that happened this morning. Eight months ago Jake brought me to Sunday school. I now know that Jesus loves me. Last week I was feeling sad about my mum in hospital, but God helped me to trust in him. I know that God's plans are the best plans. This morning my mum and dad are with me in church. Mum is feeling better and we are all here together as a family. That's what I'm going to thank God for today."

Daniel walked back to his seat and

Jake noticed that Daniel's dad was smiling proudly. Soon the service was over. As Jake walked out the door Timothy came over to chat to him. "I'm off home this afternoon. Mum has come to pick me up. She's really angry."

"I'm sorry, Tim. But you shouldn't have been smoking. You know that."

Tim nodded and looked ashamed. Jake wondered what he could say that would make things turn out right. All he could think of was, "Look, you know that I'm your friend whatever happens. If you're feeling lonely phone me."

Timothy nodded. "Yeah, I will. I

promise." Then he asked Jake to do something for him. "Could you pray for me?"

Jake patted his friend on the back. "Sure. I'll pray that God helps you to make the right choices and find some good friends."

With that Timothy turned towards his aunt who was waiting at the car. "I'd better go, but before I do, Mum said that you could come to stay with us in the summer. Would you like that?"

"Would I like that?" Jake exclaimed. "I'd love it!"

Jake ran back to speak to his mum.

She smiled when she heard Jake's news and this time she ruffled his hair. "You did well today, Jake. I think you're growing up. You've been praying and reading your Bible. You've worked so hard on that garden and it looks excellent. Let's pray that you'll be a good example for Timothy. I think he needs one right now."

Jake nodded and as he climbed in the car he said a quick prayer for Timothy and for himself.

Health

God has given us our bodies and we should look after them. We should eat healthy foods, take exercise and not do things that will harm our bodies. Sometimes that is a lesson that is hard to learn. If you're not sure about what this means you should ask a parent or a teacher for advice. Eating healthy foods does not mean that you will never eat sweets again. It doesn't mean that you have to go hungry. God gives us food. We should eat the food that our bodies need and not waste it, and we should thank God for it. It is wrong to think that the only reason for being healthy is to look good on the outside. Looking good on the outside is not as important as being healthy and is definitely not as important as having a beautiful nature and godly character.

Pray for other countries like the Sudan where they have famine and drought. Many children today have to travel for miles to collect water which is dirty and full of disease. Pray that the adults in charge of the Sudan will learn to be wise and stop fighting so that children can live healthy and happy lives.

Sickness

God heals sick people. In the Bible he healed diseases and brought people back to life. Today he gives doctors and nurses the skills to help cure diseases and he still does miracles and astonishing things. Perhaps you are asking God to heal someone but he hasn't done it yet? Remember that God's plans are not like our plans. God's plans are perfect. He knows what is best. Sometimes the best is just not what we want. If you are ill, ask someone to pray with you. Ask God to help you and to heal you and to show you what he wants to do with your life. If you know someone who is ill, pray that God would make them better. Pray that if God has a better plan he will help you and your friend to thank him in everything. Most of all, ask God to heal your soul and to make you love him with all your heart. That is the very best healing that God can do for you. Everyone is a sinner and everyone needs God's love. God's love lasts forever and his love is stronger than death.

Sarah & Paul

Written by Derek Prime

Find out about the Christian Faith with these stories of the Sarah and Paul and their friends.

Sarah & Paul
go back to *School*
Discover about God and the Bible
ISBN 1 87167 6185

Sarah & Paul
have a *Visitor*
Discover the Lord Jesus
ISBN 1 87167 6193

Sarah & Paul
go to the *Seaside*
Discover the Holy Spirit and the Church
ISBN 1 87167 6347

Sarah & Paul
make a *Scrapbook*
Discover the Lord's Prayer
ISBN 1 87167 6355

Sarah & Paul
go to the *Museum*
Discover the ten Commandments
ISBN 1 87167 6363

Sarah & Paul
on *Holiday Again*
Discover about becoming a Christian
ISBN 1 87167 6371

Look out for other stories from Canterbury Place

The Big Green
Tree at No. 11

Tammy and Jake
learn about
Life and Death

ISBN 1-85792-731-1

The Dark Blue
Bike at No. 17

Tammy and Jake
learn about
Friendship and
Bullying

ISBN 1-85792-732-X

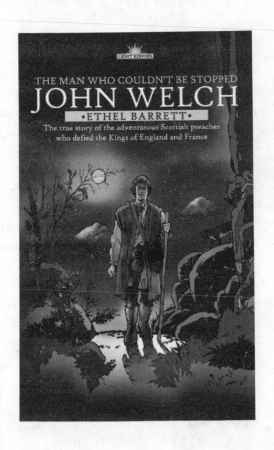

THE MAN WHO COULDN'T BE STOPPED

JOHN WELCH

•ETHEL BARRETT•

The true story of the adventurous Scottish preacher
who defied the Kings of England and France

New Lightkeepers Material!
JOHN WELCH

John Welch just couldn't be stopped.
When he was a boy he was independent, stubborn and had a mind of his own. It all ended in tears as he ran away from his father, fell in with a gang of thieves and began a life of stealing and robbery. It seemed as though he had chosen his life and nothing and no one could stop him. But then he met God. John left his sinful life and became a preacher and with God beside him there was nothing and no one who could stand in his way – not even the King of England or the King of France!
This is the true story of one of Scotland's most adventurous preachers.
As the son-in-law of another fiery Scot – John Knox – John Welch was bound to cause a stir – and he did! Find out about how he conquered roughians, saved a town from the dreaded plague and even dodged a cannon ball!

Extra Features include:
Maps, Quiz, Time Line, What was life like then?
And Fact Summaries

ISBN :1-85792-928-4

CHRISTIAN FOCUS

Staying faithful - Reaching out!

Christian Focus Publications publishes books for adults and children under its three main imprints: Christian Focus, Mentor and Christian Heritage. Our books reflect that God's word is reliable and Jesus is the way to know him, and live for ever with him.

Our children's publication list includes a Sunday school curriculum that covers pre-school to early teens; puzzle and activity books. We also publish personal and family devotional titles, biographies and inspirational stories that children will love.

If you are looking for quality Bible teaching for children then we have an excellent range of Bible story and age specific theological books.

From pre-school to teenage fiction, we have it covered!

Find us at our web page:
www.christianfocus.com